This Book Belongs To:

Lilith Livy Nottage

Date & Grade:

11/14/14   2nd

OUR MISSION

The mission of The 2nd & 7 Foundation is to promote reading by providing free books and positive role models to kids in need while encouraging young athletes in the community to pay it forward.

THANK YOU!

The Hog Mollies Writing Crew (Amy Hoying, Leah Miller, Megan McCabe)
The Ohio State University Department of Athletics • Participating Elementary Schools Teachers & Principals • 2nd & 7 Board of Directors • Current & Former Student-Athlete Readers • 2nd & 7 Football Camp Participants & Volunteers • 2nd & 7 Celebrity 8-Ball Shootout Participants & Volunteers • Countless Individual Donors

Satellite Programs and their Ambassadors, including:
Florida Atlantic University Department of Athletics • Eastern Michigan University Department of Athletics • The University of Mount Union Department of Athletics • The University of Illinois Department of Athletics • Ohio Wesleyan University • Kent State University • United Way of Henry County • Lancaster, Ohio • Albequerque, New Mexico • Betty Fairfax High School • Laveen, Arizona • Olentangy Orange High School, Lewis Center, Ohio • Mansfield City Schools

Reading Program Partners:
White Castle • Giant Eagle • Roosters • TransCounty Title Agency • The Columbus Dispatch

Thank you for sharing our passion for reading.
We hope you enjoy our 7th book!

Luke Fickell

Ryan Miller
Co-founders, The 2nd & 7 Foundation

Mike Vrabel

Cover and Interior Illustrations © 2014 Jason Tharp
The Hog Mollies & The Big Birthday Bash. Copyright © 2014 by The 2nd and 7 Foundation

ISBN 978-1-4652-4765-0
ISBN 978-1-4652-4766-7

Printed in the United States of America

Production Date: 04/15/14
Batch numbers: 43476501, 43476601
Printed by: Walsworth, Marceline, MO ; United States of America

10 9 8 7 6 5 4 3 2 1   18 17 16 15 14

TACKLING ILLITERACY

Our Tackling Illiteracy Program gives local high school, collegiate and professional athletes the opportunity to give back to their community by reading our Hog Mollies books to 2nd graders in elementary schools across the country. After these student-athletes read, they give each child a free book provided by The 2nd & 7 Foundation.

GET INVOLVED

If you are interested in learning more about how you can bring The 2nd & 7 Foundation and our Tackling Illiteracy Program to your community, email us at info@secondandseven.com or visit our website at www.secondandseven.com.

STAY CONNECTED

Follow us on Twitter or 'Like' us on Facebook to stay connected to our Tackling Illiteracy efforts.
www.twitter.com/secondandseven
www.facebook.com/The2ndand7Foundation

SECONDANDSEVEN
FOUNDATION

The 2nd & 7 Foundation is a non-profit organization based in Columbus, Ohio.
7949 N. High Street, Suite A, Columbus, Ohio 43221

The Hog Mollies

and the
Big Birthday Bash

Written by: The 2nd & 7 Foundation
Illustrated by: Jason Tharp

SECOND AND SEVEN
F O U N D A T I O N

Kendall Hunt
publishing company
4050 Westmark Drive • P O Box 1840 • Dubuque IA 52004-1840

"Hi Hog Mollies! Welcome to Majors, the best miniature golf course in town." Majors was Jackie's place, and he ran it with his wife, Barbie. "Hoppy, we're so glad you chose to celebrate your birthday here with us," Barbie added

"So am I," Hoppy said. "Did you hear who is joining us today? Bunker! He's one of the best miniature golfers around"

"Oh yes," Jackie answered. "We've ALL heard about Bunker. Now, I want to remind you to have fun today, play a good game and be a **GREAT** sport."

As the Hog Mollies chose their clubs,
Bunker arrived at the course.

The Hog Mollies - Hoppy, Duke, Harley and Sprout - gathered their friends to kick off the festivities.

"C'mon everyone, let's sing to Hoppy and have cake before we start the game," Harley suggested.

Ignoring the celebration, Bunker hurried off to make sure he was first in line at the tee.

As the Hog Mollies played their round and recorded their strokes, they noticed that some scores were better than others. But no matter what, everyone had a blast on each hole.

Everyone but Bunker. The only thing he cared about was having the best score, even if it meant being dishonest.

On the waterfall hole, everyone was met with a challenge. Feeling frustrated with his extra strokes, Bunker nudged the ball into the cup when no one was looking.

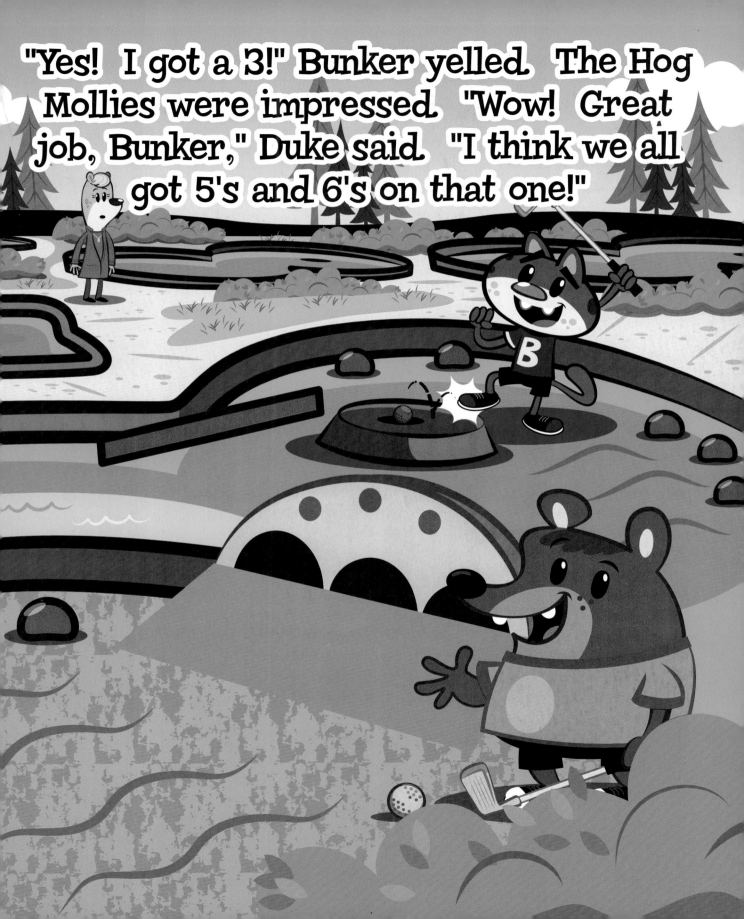

Harley missed a close shot on the shamrock hole. "Ha! You need to watch me, Harley. You could learn a lot from MY form and expertise! I would NEVER miss a shot like that." Harley's feelings were hurt by Bunker's harsh words.

"That's ok, Harley," Hoppy said. "You'll do better next time." "Don't let one hole get you down," Sprout added. "We still have a lot more golf to play."

Later in the round, Hoppy made a great shot - it banked three times before going in the hole! As he ran to give his friends a high-five, he noticed that Bunker wasn't there.

"Where's Bunker?" Sprout asked. "We haven't even finished this hole yet." "Yeah," added Harley, "I thought we were supposed to wait for everyone to make their putt before moving on."

As the Hog Mollies approached the last few holes, they began to wonder why they invited Bunker in the first place. They were having fun celebrating Hoppy's birthday, but all Bunker seemed to care about was winning.

After the round was over, the gang reviewed their scorecard to see who had the fewest strokes.

OFFICIAL SCORECARD
HOLES 10–18

HOPPY	2	3	2	1	3	4	2	4	3
DUKE	4	2	3	2	1	2	3	3	2
SPROUT	2	2	4	2	3	1	2	4	4
HARLEY	3	4	5	3	2	4	3	2	2
BUNKER	2	1	1	1	2	2	2	1	2

PLAY A GOOD GAME, BE A GREAT SPORT.

Jackie and Barbie greeted the party guests at the last hole. "Wow! Great game everyone. It looked like you had a fun round"

"We sure did! Thanks for a fun party," Hoppy said. "Bunker was the big winner. It looks like he's the best player."

"Actually, Hoppy, Bunker may have had the best score, but you and the rest of the Hog Mollies played a better game."

"What are you talking about?! I had the best round!" Bunker protested.

"Bunker, being a good sport means waiting your turn, taking care of the course, respecting the other players, and being honest," Barbie reminded him. "Just like the Hog Mollies did today."

"It's not always the scorecard that counts. The Hog Mollies were the winners today, because at Majors, the most important thing is sportsmanship."

Play a good game, be a GREAT SPORT

Sportsmanship and Golf Etiquette for Kids

Whether you are on the links or a miniature golf course, here are a few helpful tips to remember. Unlike most other competitive sports, golf is played without supervision or a referee, so it is up to each player to be courteous, honest, fair and respectful--all traits of a GOOD SPORT!

1. Be as quiet as possible when others are taking their turn to avoid disrupting their shot.

2. The player whose ball is furthest away from the hole always goes first.

3. Wait for all players in your group to complete each hole before moving on to the next one.

4. Always be respectful of the course and other golfers.

5. At the end of the round, shake hands with your fellow players; congratulate the winners and console the losers.

6. Remember that golf is a game and is meant to be FUN!

Play a GOOD game; be a GREAT sport!

I was a GREAT sport when . . .

_____

_____

_____

_____

_____

_____

_____

_____